A Mystery
from the Past

Dirt was flying everywhere, and the only part of their sheepdog puppy that the Bobbsey twins could see was his wagging tail. The rest of him was busily digging a huge hole in the ground.

"Look! Chief's found something," Freddie said.

Finally, Chief backed out of the hole, dragging a dirt-covered object in his mouth.

Bert knelt down for a closer look. "It's a bone," he told the others.

"What kind of bone?" Nan asked.

The twins stared at one another. Then Flossie spoke up. "Do you think it could be a *human* bone?"

Books in The New Bobbsey Twins series

Available from MINSTREL Books

THE NEW
Bobbsey Twins

#16 Twins™

THE CASE OF THE DISAPPEARING DINOSAUR

LAURA LEE HOPE

ILLUSTRATED BY PAUL JENNIS

A MINSTREL® BOOK

PUBLISHED BY POCKET BOOKS

New York   London   Toronto   Sydney   Tokyo   Singapore

A MINSTREL PAPERBACK *ORIGINAL*

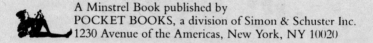

A Minstrel Book published by
POCKET BOOKS, a division of Simon & Schuster Inc.
1230 Avenue of the Americas, New York, NY 10020

ISBN: 0-671-67597-4

First Minstrel Books printing February 1990

10 9 8 7 6 5 4 3 2 1

Contents

THE CASE OF THE DISAPPEARING DINOSAUR

1
Making Plans

"Chief needs his own room," Flossie Bobbsey announced. She was lying on the living-room floor, using the family's lovable sheepdog puppy as a pillow.

Freddie Bobbsey rolled his eyes at his blond, blue-eyed twin. "That's silly," he said. "Dogs don't have rooms, they have doghouses."

"Okay," Flossie said. "Chief needs a doghouse, then."

"Where will you find one big enough for him?" Freddie asked. Chief was going to be a very large dog.

"We can make him one." Flossie looked over at her older brother and sister. "Can't we?"

"I don't know, Flossie," twelve-year-old Nan said. "Building a doghouse could be a lot of work."

"But we're Chief's family. We have to take care of him," Flossie said. "If we all work together, it won't be so hard."

"Maybe she's right," Bert said. He was Nan's twin. Bert and Nan had brown hair and brown eyes. "We could design the plans ourselves and get wood from Dad's lumberyard."

"I bet Dad will help us," Nan said. "Besides, if Chief has a doghouse, then he won't sleep on our sofa. Right, Chief?"

Nan reached over and scratched Chief behind one ear. The sheepdog gave a happy sigh.

"Of course Dad will help," Flossie said, beaming. "He loves Chief, too."

"You know, this project could really be fun." Bert was starting to like the idea.

"The first thing we should do is find out how big Chief is," Freddie said. "I mean, what good is a doghouse if it doesn't fit the dog?"

Freddie ran and got his tape measure. He and Bert gently stretched Chief out and measured him from the tip of his nose to the end of his tail. Then they measured how wide he was.

Meanwhile, Nan pulled out her sketch pad. Flossie started describing the kind of house she thought Chief would like. Nan drew a sketch.

Flossie frowned. "I don't think that's fancy enough."

Nan drew another sketch. "How's this?"

Flossie shook her head. "The doorway is too small."

Pretty soon the floor was covered with crumpled-up pieces of drawing paper.

"This is the last one," Nan warned her sister.

Flossie studied Nan's sketch. Finally, she nodded. "It's perfect!"

Flossie showed the sketch to Chief. The others laughed, but they had to admit that their pet looked pleased.

Then Bert took the sketch. He made a plan for how to build the doghouse, using the measurements he and Freddie had taken.

After dinner the twins showed Mr. and Mrs. Bobbsey their plans. "This is very good," Mr. Bobbsey said. He sounded really impressed.

Mrs. Bobbsey nodded in agreement. "It's about time Chief had a doghouse." At the sound of his name, Chief trotted over, wagging his tail.

Mr. Bobbsey went over the plans very carefully with the twins. Then he helped them figure out how much lumber they would need.

"Why don't you come over to the lumberyard tomorrow after school," Mr. Bobbsey suggested. "You can pick up what you'll need to get started."

Flossie knelt down and threw her arms around Chief. "We're going to build you the most beautiful doghouse in Lakeport," she promised.

"Woof!" Chief barked happily.

The next day, Freddie, Bert, and Nan were getting ready to go to their father's lumberyard. Flossie appeared with Chief's leash.

"Why are you carrying that?" Nan asked suspiciously.

"For Chief, of course," Flossie explained.

"He can't come," Freddie said. "He'll run around the lumberyard and get into trouble."

"Freddie's right, Floss," Bert said. "It's not a good idea to bring him with us."

"But it's his doghouse!" Flossie wailed. "There might be special pieces of wood he wants us to use. How will we know if he doesn't come?"

"Well, maybe it'll be okay to bring him this time," Nan said. "But you'll have to hold on to his leash."

Flossie smiled. "Don't worry. I will."

"Okay, that's settled," Bert said. "Let's get going."

"I brought my camera," Flossie said as they headed out the door. "I want to take pictures of Chief's house, right from the beginning. Then I'll make him a scrapbook."

"Oh, brother," Freddie said, rolling his eyes.

The twins got on their bikes and pedaled to the lumberyard. Chief rode in Nan's basket.

The lumberyard was one of the twins' favorite places. The smell of freshly cut wood hung in the air. The wood was cut in many shapes and sizes. It was carefully stacked in piles all around the yard.

As soon as they'd parked their bikes, the twins went straight to their father's office. Mr. Bobbsey was sitting at his desk, talking with Sam Johnson. Sam had worked at the lumberyard for as long as the twins could remember.

"Show Sam your plans," Mr. Bobbsey told the twins after they had said hello.

The twins carefully spread out Nan's sketch

and Bert's measurements on the desk. Sam studied the paper, then looked up.

"These are great!" he said. He patted Chief's back. "You're a lucky dog." Chief licked his hand.

While Mr. Bobbsey left to help some customers, Sam looked at the plans more closely. He wanted to see exactly what size pieces of wood the twins would need. He also made some suggestions on the best way for them to build the doghouse.

The twins were so busy, they forgot about Chief. When they were ready to go outside to choose the actual boards for the doghouse, Flossie noticed the dog was gone.

"Where's Chief?" she asked the others. "I think he should sniff the boards to make sure he likes them."

Nan turned to her sister. "I thought you were going to hold on to him."

Flossie looked uncomfortable. "Well, I was," she said in a small voice. "I guess I dropped his leash."

"I hope he hasn't gotten into any trouble," Mr. Bobbsey said, coming through the door.

"I'll go look for him," Freddie offered. He raced out of the office and ran through the

lumberyard, calling Chief's name. At first, there was no answering bark. Then the other twins heard Chief barking excitedly.

"Over here!" they heard Freddie shout. "By the back fence. Hurry!"

"It sounds like Chief is in trouble!" cried Flossie.

The twins ran to the back fence. Dirt was flying everywhere, and the only part of Chief they could see was his tail. It was wagging frantically back and forth. The rest of him was busily digging a huge hole in the ground.

"Uh-oh," Nan said. "Dad's not going to like this."

"Look! Chief found something," Freddie said.

"Maybe it's buried treasure," said Flossie.

Whatever Chief had uncovered seemed to be very large. Finally, he backed out of the hole, dragging something in his mouth.

"What is that?" Freddie asked.

"Whatever it is, it's covered with dirt," said Flossie. "Yuck!"

Bert knelt down and helped the dog pull out his prize.

It was a very large bone. Bert examined it and then placed it on the ground.

"What kind of bone is that?" asked Nan.

"I don't know," Bert said, looking puzzled. "It's enormous."

The twins all stared at the bone. Then Flossie said, "Do you think it could be a *human* bone?"

2
The Mystery Bone

"Don't be silly," Nan said firmly. "The bone must be from some sort of animal, that's all."

"How do you *know* that?" Flossie demanded.

"Yeah," said Freddie. "You don't know everything about bones."

Just then Mr. Bobbsey and Sam rushed up.

"What was all the noise about?" Mr. Bobbsey asked.

"Look at the size of that hole!" Sam exclaimed. He shook his finger at the dog. "You're in trouble this time, Chief."

"But wait till you see what he found!" Freddie cried.

The twins showed their father and Sam the bone. The two men had to admit that it was very strange looking.

Freddie turned to Bert. "I bet it *is* human."

"No," Sam said. "It's much too big to have come from a person."

"Well, maybe the person was a giant," Flossie insisted. The others burst out laughing.

"There must be someone who can tell us what kind of bone it is," Nan said.

"Why don't we call the zoo?" Mr. Bobbsey suggested.

"Right!" Bert agreed. "They're used to people asking all kinds of questions."

Mr. Bobbsey picked up the bone with both hands and headed back to the office. Everyone followed behind him. Chief trotted alongside Mr. Bobbsey. He never took his eyes off the bone.

When they got to the office, the twins' father wiped off the bone with a cloth, then put the bone carefully on the desk. Chief sat down in the doorway. He was guarding the bone.

Bert made the call to the zoo. The woman he spoke to sounded very interested in the bone. Bert tried to tell her what the bone looked like.

It wasn't easy. Every time Bert lifted the bone to see it better, Chief growled at him.

"We can send Dr. Willa Hayes to look at the bone," the woman told Bert. "She's a zoologist—she knows all about animals. Will it be all right if she comes by tomorrow morning?"

Bert repeated the question to his father, who nodded yes. Then Bert promised the woman, "Don't worry. We'll take good care of the bone. 'Bye!"

The twins were all very excited. "I knew the bone was important!" Freddie said. "I bet this turns out to be a big discovery."

"Chief! You'll be famous!" Flossie hugged the shaggy dog.

"Maybe we should do some investigating before Dr. Hayes gets here tomorrow," Bert said.

He pulled a magnifying glass from his pocket and peered at the bone.

"It's not totally smooth," he reported. "There are lines running up and down and across the bone." He handed the magnifying glass to Nan.

"I see what you mean," she said, squinting through the glass. "I wonder what made those lines."

Bert shrugged. "Maybe Dr. Hayes can answer that question."

"I'm going to make a sketch of the bone," said Nan. She found some paper and drew the bone from several angles.

"I'll take a picture of the bone next to this ruler on Dad's desk," Freddie said. He turned to Flossie. "May I please borrow your camera?" he asked politely.

Flossie grinned and handed it to him. "Just make sure you point it in the right direction," she teased.

Freddie snapped a couple of photos. Then he suggested. "Let's go back to the hole. We should take pictures of where Chief found the bone."

Bert carefully picked up the bone, and the twins headed for the back fence. Chief kept jumping up at the bone.

Freddie walked all around the hole that Chief had dug. He took two pictures of the hole, then he snapped some more photographs of the bone. Then he picked up the bone and placed it back into the hole.

"Hey, what are you doing?" Bert asked.

Chief started barking and went after his

bone. Flossie grabbed the dog's collar and held on to it tightly. Chief squirmed and barked again.

"I told you before that you have to get pictures of the bone in the place it was discovered," Freddie explained. "I read it in a book called *The Scientific Detectives*."

Flossie held Chief while Freddie took his pictures. He managed to take two before Chief broke free and jumped back into the hole to rescue his bone. The sheepdog came bounding out, dragging the bone. He almost knocked Freddie over in his excitement.

Just then Sam came over and told the twins that it was closing time. "Your father is waiting for you to bring the bone back to the office," Sam added.

Mr. Bobbsey had found a long box and put some newspapers in it. He and Bert carefully laid the bone inside, put the lid on, and pushed the box next to Mr. Bobbsey's desk. Then they all left the office.

The lumberyard workers and the last customers were leaving. Mr. Bobbsey stood by the gate, smiling and saying goodbye. Sam pulled out his key ring and got ready to lock up.

"Maybe our picture will be in the newspaper

for making a scientific discovery," Freddie said.

"You mean, maybe *Chief's* picture will be in the paper," Flossie reminded her twin. "After all, it was his discovery."

Nan laughed. "Maybe we should take a picture of him in case the newspaper doesn't."

Freddie bit his lip. "Uh, I'm not sure where I left the camera," he admitted.

"I can't believe it!" said Flossie. "You lost my camera!"

"Don't get excited," Freddie said. "It's probably in the office." He ran back to the office. Sam hadn't locked the door yet, so Freddie looked inside.

Moments later he was back at the gate. "Nope, it's not there," he said. "But it has to be around here somewhere."

"It better be," Flossie muttered.

"Let's all look," Sam said. "The sooner we find it, the sooner we can go home."

"Should we take Chief with us?" asked Flossie.

Mr. Bobbsey looked at the sheepdog. Chief was lying on the ground, fast asleep.

"I think we can leave him here by himself," the twins' father said. "He's probably pretty tired out from all the excitement."

The search for the camera took awhile. Finally, Freddie found it. He had put it down on a pile of doors and forgotten it.

When they all got back to the gate, Chief was waiting for them.

"I'll take Chief's picture," Flossie said, grabbing her camera from Freddie. "That will finish the roll. We can drop off the film at the Photo-Fast camera store on the way home. They have overnight developing."

"Right," Mr. Bobbsey said. "Let's go." He waited until Sam and the twins had gone through the gate. Then he pulled the gate shut and locked it. The lumberyard was closed for the night.

The next day was Saturday. That morning the twins were ready to leave for the lumberyard even before Mr. Bobbsey had finished his breakfast.

"What if Dr. Hayes is there already?" Flossie said. "Nobody will be at the lumberyard to let her in."

"Calm down, Flossie," said Mr. Bobbsey. "I'm sure you'll get to the lumberyard before she does. It's still pretty early."

"I'll get Chief," Flossie said.

"I don't think he has to come this morning," Mr. Bobbsey said. "Things run a little more smoothly at the lumberyard without him."

"But what if Dr. Hayes wants to meet him?" Flossie asked.

"We'll be sure to give Chief all the credit," Nan said.

"I'll bike over and pick up our pictures on the way," Freddie said. "Then we can show Dr. Hayes what Chief looks like."

Flossie brightened a little. "Okay."

Freddie headed for the camera shop, and the others got into Mr. Bobbsey's car. When they reached the lumberyard, Bert, Nan, and Flossie hurried into the office.

"Look!" Nan gasped. She pointed to the box next to Mr. Bobbsey's desk.

Everyone stared. The top had been knocked off—and the box was empty.

The mysterious bone was gone!

3
Stolen!

"We've been robbed!" cried Flossie.

"This is crazy," said Nan. "Who would want to steal a bone?"

Mr. Bobbsey started to pick up the empty box.

"Wait," Flossie said. "You shouldn't disturb the scene of the crime. At least not until there's been a proper investigation."

Mr. Bobbsey straightened up and smiled. "You're absolutely right, Flossie," he said. "I wasn't thinking like a detective."

"We'd better call the police," Sam said.

"Why do we need the police?" Flossie said. "We're the first people at the scene of the crime, and we know the bone the best. Why shouldn't we investigate?"

"I can think of a couple of reasons," Mr. Bobbsey began. "For one thing, if someone took the trouble to steal the bone, it just might be valuable."

"Maybe Dr. Hayes will be able to tell us about the bone," Bert said. "We can show her the photos we took."

"All right," said Mr. Bobbsey. "But after we talk to her, we'll call the police."

Before anyone could reply, they heard a woman's voice calling, "Hello! Is anyone there?"

"That must be Dr. Hayes," Sam said.

A red-haired woman wearing glasses appeared at the door. "I'm Dr. Willa Hayes," she said. "Are you the Bobbseys?"

Mr. Bobbsey introduced himself, the twins, and Sam to Dr. Hayes.

Dr. Hayes smiled. "I came to see the bone you discovered. It sounds very interesting."

The Bobbseys and Sam looked at one another. Then Bert said, "We can't show it to you right now."

"Why not?" asked Dr. Hayes. She looked puzzled.

"It seems to have been—" began Nan.

"Stolen!" finished Flossie. "Somebody came here in the middle of the night and took the bone."

Dr. Hayes looked very surprised. "But who would do such a thing?" she asked.

"We don't know," said Bert. "But we're going to find out."

"Find out what?" Freddie asked from the doorway. He was breathing heavily after rushing from the camera store to the lumberyard.

"Oh, Freddie!" said Flossie. "Someone stole the bone!"

"Have you searched for clues yet?" Freddie asked the other twins.

"Before you start your investigation," said Dr. Hayes, "maybe you could help me start mine. Can you describe the bone to me?"

"We can do better than that," Freddie said. "We can show you photos. I looked at them in the camera store, and they came out great. I had some copies made, too."

The first five photos had been taken by Flossie at a friend's birthday party. The rest were from the day before. The photos showed the bone, the hole, and the bone in the hole.

"We even took the picture of the bone with a

ruler next to it, so that you could see how long the bone is."

"These are excellent, Freddie." Dr. Hayes sounded impressed. "How did you know to take a picture with a ruler? It really helps."

"A book I read said that when scientists find dinosaur bones, they always take pictures with rulers," Freddie told her. "So they have an official record of how big the bones are."

"You've done good work," Dr. Hayes said.

Freddie grinned proudly.

"And who is this?" Dr. Hayes pointed to the last two pictures.

"That's Chief," Nan said. "He's the one who actually found the bone. Flossie thinks he'll be famous."

"You never know," said Willa Hayes. "Well, I'm convinced that you've found an unusual bone. I guess I'd better call the zoology department at the university. I need some extra help on this one."

"You don't need any extra help," Freddie said.

"What do you mean, Freddie?" asked Nan.

Freddie smiled. "I know where the bone came from," he said. "A dinosaur."

The other twins laughed. Even Mr. Bobbsey

and Sam began to chuckle. Everyone was laughing except Freddie and Dr. Hayes.

"You know," Dr. Hayes said slowly, "I think Freddie may be right."

The other Bobbseys and Sam stared at Freddie.

"A dinosaur bone? Nan asked.

"Uh-huh," said Freddie. "Did you know that *dinosaur* means terrible lizard? Millions of years ago, dinosaurs lived everywhere—even here in Lakeport."

"It's hard to imagine that," Nan said.

"Actually, several dinosaur bones have been discovered in this area," said Dr. Hayes.

"Chief really will be famous," Flossie said, her eyes shining.

"You might all be famous," Dr. Hayes said cheerfully.

"*If* we can find the bone again," Bert reminded her.

"Well, I think it's time to call the police." Mr. Bobbsey reached for the phone.

"But we can solve this ourselves," Bert said to his father. "I know we can."

"We've solved a lot of cases already," Nan explained to Dr. Hayes.

"I still think I'd better report the theft," said Mr. Bobbsey.

After he hung up the phone, Mr. Bobbsey explained that the police needed to know exactly what kind of bone was missing. "They'd like you to call them, as soon as you've identified the bone," Mr. Bobbsey said to Dr. Hayes.

"I will," promised Dr. Hayes.

"I'm going to get to work," Sam said.

Mr. Bobbsey nodded. "I'll join you in a moment," he said as Sam went out into the lumberyard.

Willa Hayes picked up the phone. "I'm going to call a professor at the university—Dr. Bob Trent. He's a paleontologist—that's someone who's an expert on ancient life, including dinosaurs."

"Be sure to tell him we have pictures," Freddie reminded her.

"And tell him that the bone had rough lines on it," Bert said.

"And don't forget to tell him how Chief dug it up," Flossie added.

"Don't worry." Willa Hayes smiled. "I'll tell him *everything*."

When Professor Trent answered the phone,

Dr. Hayes began describing the bone and how the Bobbseys had found it.

All of a sudden Willa Hayes looked very upset. "You must be mistaken, Professor Trent," she said. "Please don't shout."

"Maybe I should tell him about the bone," Freddie said. "After all, I took the pictures of it."

Dr. Hayes handed Freddie the phone. He listened for a minute. "But—" he began. "But we—" he repeated. Then he held the phone away from his ear. Professor Trent was yelling so loudly they all could hear him.

"Young man!" he shouted. "You have stolen my dinosaur bone, and I am going to report you to the police. You're nothing but a bunch of thieves! All of you!"

4

Professor Trent's Dinosaur

"But, Professor," Freddie tried again. "My name is Freddie Bobbsey. I'm the one who discovered the bone." Freddie glanced at Flossie. "I mean I was the first person to get there after our dog, Chief, found the bone. And we didn't steal the bone, we tried to save it."

Freddie moved the phone away from his ear. Professor Trent was still talking loudly enough for all the Bobbseys to hear him.

"A dog discovered that bone, you say? Nonsense! I am the discoverer of that dinosaur bone!"

"He sounds pretty upset," Flossie said.

"Well, at least we know now that it probably *is* a dinosaur bone," said Bert.

Mr. Bobbsey took the phone. He looked angry. "Professor Trent, this is Richard Bobbsey. I own the lumberyard where the bone was found. My children didn't steal your bone. Someone else did. In fact, they're going to start looking for it. I'm sure your bone will be found."

Professor Trent began yelling again. "Listen, I have already reported the theft to the police. I am now going to call them back and tell them that I discovered the thieves!" There was a loud click as Professor Trent slammed down the phone.

Mr. Bobbsey hung up the phone and frowned. "I wonder if he always acts that way."

"Where's Dr. Hayes?" Bert asked, looking around. "Maybe she can tell us more about Professor Trent."

"Yeah," said Freddie, "so we can see if he's always crazy, or if he's just upset because he lost his bone."

"That's weird," said Nan. "Dr. Hayes was just here, and now she's gone." Nan stuck her head out of the office. "I don't see her," she said. "I'll go look around."

"I'll come with you," Mr. Bobbsey said. He and Nan disappeared into the lumberyard.

Bert, Flossie, and Freddie continued to search for clues. "Look at this," Bert said. He picked up a piece of cardboard from the floor. It matched the cardboard of the box the bone had been in.

"Why would someone rip off a piece of the cardboard?" Bert asked. "The box wasn't sealed."

Before anyone could answer, Nan came back into the office. "Dr. Hayes is gone," she announced. "Dad and I searched the whole lumberyard."

"That's funny," said Freddie. "She seemed so interested in the bone."

"Look." Flossie pointed out the window.

A police car had pulled into the lumberyard parking lot, and Lieutenant Pike was getting out. The twins knew Lieutenant Pike from other mysteries they had solved. Mr. Bobbsey came into the parking lot and shook the lieutenant's hand. A man wearing a rumpled jacket and a bow tie got out of the passenger side of the police car and joined the two men. The twins saw Lieutenant Pike introduce him to Mr. Bobbsey.

"I bet they're here to investigate our bone," Flossie said.

The twins hurried out of the office. When they got to the parking lot, Lieutenant Pike greeted them with a smile.

"I hear you kids found a bone," he said. "And lost it."

"Something like that," Freddie said.

"There's someone here who wants to meet you, Freddie." Lieutenant Pike turned to the man standing next to him. "This is Professor Trent. I think you've already talked to him on the phone."

"Sort of," Freddie said.

"I want to apologize for having yelled at you," Professor Trent said. "I'm afraid I have quite a temper. But I was very upset."

"We could tell," Flossie said.

"It's just that this bone means a great deal to me," Dr. Trent explained. "It is a very important scientific discovery."

"See?" Freddie said. "I told you it was important."

"Well, you were right," Professor Trent told Freddie. "It is from the right front leg of a Diplodocus. That was a very large, very beautiful dinosaur. It lived around here millions of years ago. Of course, that was when this was all jungle."

"Jungle?" Nan said, surprised.

"Oh, yes," said Professor Trent. "The earth's climate was very different then. Huge dinosaurs like the Diplodocus lived in this area. I didn't think I'd ever be able to put together a whole skeleton. Not until I discovered that bone. And now it's missing! So you can see why I'm so upset."

"Were those diplo-whatevers really big?" asked Flossie.

"Oh, yes," said Professor Trent. "The Diplodocus was so tall that it could stand in thirty feet of water and still stick its head out."

"Wow!" Flossie said. "That's tall."

"I explained to Professor Trent that you kids are pretty sharp detectives," Lieutenant Pike said.

"That's why I came to talk to you," Professor Trent said. "I want you to find out who stole my bone. But I'm in a great hurry. Scientists from all over the world will be meeting at the university very soon. I want to show them my finished skeleton," he explained.

"Well, first we have to make sure that the

bone Chief found really is the bone that you lost," Nan said.

"Right," said Freddie. "You'd better take a look at my photographs. They're in Dad's office."

"Lead the way," said the professor.

"I think I'll go and take a look at where the bone was found," said Lieutenant Pike.

"I'll show you where the hole is," Bert offered. He and Lieutenant Pike set off for the back fence.

Mr. Bobbsey went to help a customer. Freddie, Flossie, Nan, and Professor Trent headed for the office.

"You know," said Nan, "it would be awful if Chief found an old cow bone after all."

"He didn't," Flossie and Freddie said together. "He found a dinosaur."

When they got to the office, Freddie handed the photographs to Professor Trent.

"These are very good, young man," Professor Trent said.

Freddie looked pleased.

"But is it the same bone?" said Nan.

"There is no doubt." Professor Trent sighed. "It's definitely the same bone that was stolen from my lab."

33

Just then there was a knock at the door. Holly McCarthy, a college student who worked part time at the lumberyard, stuck her head into the office.

"Hi, everybody," she said with a smile. "Is Mr. Bobbsey here? I have some papers for him."

"I'll put them on his desk for you," Nan said. She took the papers Holly was holding. Just then Professor Trent looked up from Freddie's pictures.

He made a strange sort of choking sound, and his face turned bright red. "It's her!" he shouted. "She's the one who stole my bone!"

5

Some Suspects

"Get Lieutenant Pike!" Professor Trent bellowed.

"He's crazy," Flossie whispered to Nan. "He thinks *everybody* stole his bone!"

Holly stepped into the office.

"I don't have anything of yours," she told Professor Trent. "*You* stole something from *me,* and you know it."

"What did he take?" Flossie asked, her eyes wide.

"How do you two know each other?" Nan asked.

But Professor Trent and Holly were too busy arguing to answer.

"You think that you already know everything," Professor Trent said to Holly. "You forget that you're only a student. You're not an expert—yet."

"Maybe I *am* just a student," Holly said. "But students know things, too. And you don't appreciate the work they do for you."

"Are you one of Professor Trent's students?" Nan broke in.

"I used to be," Holly said.

Dr. Trent cleared his throat. "If we could get back to my missing dinosaur bone, which this young lady stole. You children won't have to play detective anymore. I'll just step outside and tell Lieutenant Pike that I've solved the case."

"Too late," Flossie said, glancing out the window. "Lieutenant Pike is leaving."

"Well, then, I'll call the station and leave a message," Professor Trent told them.

"Wait a minute," Nan said. "What proof do you have that Holly stole your bone?"

"Don't worry, I'll get proof," Professor Trent said.

"Well, can you tell us why you suspect Holly?" Nan asked. "Maybe we could help."

"I don't need your help. I *know* that she's

guilty." Dr. Trent glared at all of them, then stormed out the door.

He bumped into Bert, who was just coming back into the office.

"What's the matter with him?" Bert asked. The others quickly told him what had happened while he'd been with Lieutenant Pike.

"I'd better get back to work," Holly said.

"Before you go," Nan said, "could we ask you a couple of questions about Professor Trent?"

"I guess so." Holly shrugged.

"What do you know about Professor Trent's dinosaur skeleton?" Nan asked.

"Well, he's been working on it for almost ten years," Holly told her. "Every summer he takes a group of students on a dig. That means they go to a place where Professor Trent thinks dinosaur bones are buried in the earth. Then they dig to try to find them.

Holly held up the photographs. "Very few bones are found in such large pieces as this one. If you look carefully, you can see very faint lines. That's where the pieces of bone were glued together."

Bert nodded. "I noticed those lines."

"You mean this bone wasn't really whole?" Freddie sounded disappointed.

"Oh, no," Holly said. "It would be unlikely to find such a big bone in one piece after so many years. It takes months of work to find the pieces and fit them together. We dig very carefully to make sure that we find the little pieces of bone. We sift all of the dirt as we dig it up. When we find pieces, we label all of them very carefully. Then we fit them together back at the university. Usually, parts of the bone are still missing, so we fill them in with cement where we have to."

"And Dr. Trent does all of that?" Bert asked.

"He's in charge," Holly said. "But it takes a lot of people to help."

"You mean the students," Nan said.

"Exactly." Holly looked at her watch. "I really do have to get back to work. I'll see you later." Holly smiled and headed out the door.

"But I wanted to ask her some dinosaur questions," Freddie said.

"You can do that when this case is over," Bert said. "First, we have to find out who stole that bone."

* * *

That evening the twins rushed to read the *Lakeport News.* Mrs. Bobbsey had said there might be a story on Chief's bone in the Saturday edition.

There was. On the third page the twins found an article about the bone. Then there was a story about Professor Trent. It mentioned the skeleton he had been working on.

"It doesn't say that Professor Trent is a mean man," Flossie said.

"He's not really mean," Nan said, trying to be fair. "He just has a terrible temper."

"Well, I think he's mean enough to steal his own bone and blame someone else," Flossie pointed out.

"Like Holly?" said Nan. "That would be an awful thing to do."

"I hate to say this," Bert said, "but Holly has to be at the top of our list of suspects."

"Not Holly," Flossie said. "She's too nice."

"But you have to admit it's a big coincidence that she works at the lumberyard," said Freddie. "And that she knows all about Professor Trent and his skeleton."

"You know," Bert said thoughtfully, "that woman from the zoo acted really weird."

"You mean Dr. Hayes," Freddie said. "She disappeared even before Professor Trent got there—almost as if she didn't want him to see her."

"That's true," Nan agreed. Before she could say anything else, the phone rang. Mr. Bobbsey picked it up.

"It's Lieutenant Pike," Mr. Bobbsey told the twins. "He wants to know if Freddie's pictures of the bone are here, and if there are copies."

"Yep," Freddie said. "They're in my room."

"Well, the police would like the copies," Mr. Bobbsey said. He talked to Lieutenant Pike for a few moments, then hung up the phone. "Lieutenant Pike is dropping by to pick them up," he said.

When the police car arrived, all the twins went to talk to Lieutenant Pike. The lieutenant took the envelope from Freddie and glanced through the pictures. "Thanks, Freddie," he said. "These will be very helpful."

"What have you found out so far?" Bert asked.

"Not much," said Lieutenant Pike. "But we're checking on the people who work at the lumberyard."

"Poor Holly." Flossie sighed.

"She isn't the only person who had a chance to take the bone," Lieutenant Pike said.

"But who would want it?" Nan asked.

"That bone is very valuable to scientists like Professor Trent. The thief might think he's willing to pay a lot of money to get the bone back."

Lieutenant Pike waved goodbye and drove off. After he was gone, the twins thought about what he had said.

"The only other person who was at the lumberyard when we locked up was Sam," Nan reminded the twins.

"The police couldn't suspect Sam." Freddie sounded horrified. "He wouldn't steal anything."

"*We* know that," Nan pointed out. "But we'd better make sure the police know it, too. After all, Sam is the only person besides Dad with a key to the lumberyard office."

"We'll have to talk to Sam," Bert said. "We need to find out where he was last night."

There was still enough time before dark to bike over to the Johnsons' house. When the twins got there, they rang the doorbell. Sam's wife, Dinah, answered their ring. She was an attractive woman with short black hair and dark brown eyes.

Dinah smiled at the twins. "How nice to see you! Why don't you come in. I just made a fresh batch of chocolate chip cookies."

"Mmm," said Flossie. "That sounds great!"

Nan gave her sister a look, as if to remind her why they were there.

"Is Sam here?" Nan asked, as they stepped into the house. "We have to talk to him right away."

"No," Dinah said. "He went bowling with some of his friends." She left the room for a moment, then returned with a plate full of cookies.

"Actually, I'm glad you came over," Dinah said. "I'm worried."

"What's the matter?" Nan asked.

"It's about that bone you found," Dinah said. "The police called to say that they want to talk to Sam about it."

"There's nothing to worry about," Bert said. "They just need to know where Sam was the night the bone was stolen."

"But that's the problem," Dinah said. "Sam won't say where he was. I was visiting my mother that night, and I called Sam a lot of times. But he didn't answer the phone until late, and he wouldn't tell me where he'd been. If he won't tell the police, either, they'll definitely think he's the thief!"

6

Where Was Sam?

Now the twins were even more worried about Sam.

"I know Sam is innocent," Flossie declared the next morning.

"Of course he's innocent!" Freddie said. "But we have to get him to tell us—and the police—where he was the other night."

"I bet Holly stole the bone," Bert said.

"Well, I hope not," Nan said. "I really like her."

"So do I," Bert replied. "But a good detective can't let feelings get in the way of an investigation."

"I know." Nan sighed. "I guess we'll just have to pretend Holly and Sam are strangers."

"Flossie and I are going to the lumberyard to talk to Sam," Freddie announced.

"Good idea," Nan said. "Bert and I will meet you there later."

When Freddie and Flossie got to the lumberyard, they looked around for Sam. He was in the back, supervising two men who were unloading a truck.

The twins ducked behind a stack of wood.

"Maybe we should get closer," Flossie whispered. "We can't really see Sam that well from here."

Freddie nodded. He and Flossie darted behind another pile of lumber. When the men moved to another part of the yard, the twins followed. They always stayed hidden.

Finally, the two workers got into their truck and drove away. Then Sam turned around. "Well, you two can come out now. They're gone."

Flossie and Freddie stood up. They felt a little silly.

"Hi, Sam," Flossie said, brushing herself off. What a lot of work for nothing!

Sam looked amused. "Who are you hiding from?" he asked.

"We weren't hiding," Freddie blurted out. "We were investigating."

"Who were you investigating?" Sam asked. The twins didn't answer. "Me?" Sam said in surprise.

"Of course not!" Flossie said quickly. She didn't want to hurt Sam's feelings. "We're on the dinosaur bone case, remember? And we need to find out where everybody was on the night the bone got stolen."

"Look, kids, I have a lot of work to do to-day," Sam said. "I don't really have time to talk to you now." Sam turned and walked away.

The twins looked at each other, alarmed. Why didn't Sam want to talk to them? Did he have something to hide?

"Sam, wait," Flossie called. She and Freddie hurried to catch up to him.

"We have to talk to you," Freddie said.

Sam stopped. "All right, but be quick. I have a lot to do."

"Just tell us where you were Friday night, and we'll stop bothering you," Flossie said.

"You think that *I* stole the bone?" Sam sounded shocked.

"*We* don't," Flossie said.

"But the police do," Freddie added.

Sam looked from one twin to the other. Then he sighed and sat down on a pile of lumber.

"I guess I'll have to explain," Sam said. "But you have to promise to keep my secret."

"Well, we might have to tell the police," Freddie pointed out.

"Let *me* tell the police, okay?" Sam said. "I planned to call them today, anyway."

"What about Bert and Nan?" Flossie asked.

"They have to promise not to tell, either," Sam said. He took a deep breath. "I was at my French lesson."

"But why didn't you tell Dinah?" Freddie said. Learning French didn't seem like such a terrible thing.

Sam shook his head. "I don't want her to know anything about it," he said. "Dinah and I are going on a vacation in a couple of months. We're going to Montreal, in Canada. The people in Montreal speak French. I thought I'd surprise Dinah by talking to everybody there in their own language."

"Wow," Flossie said. "I bet she'll be really proud of you."

"I hope so," Sam said. "Because this trip is an anniversary present. I want everything to be perfect. So remember not to tell anyone except Bert and Nan," Sam added. "I don't want to ruin the surprise."

The twins agreed, and Sam stood up. "Now I really do have to finish my work. I have a lesson later with Monsieur Berne."

"Thanks for telling us, Sam," said Freddie.

"No problem," Sam said. He smiled at the twins and walked away.

"Well, let's get going," Freddie said.

"Where?" asked Flossie.

"To check out Sam's story," Freddie said impatiently.

"Freddie!" Flossie said, shocked. "You mean you don't believe Sam?"

"Well, I do believe Sam, but if it was anybody else I might not. I would find out if the story was true," Freddie said.

"I guess you're right," Flossie said with a sigh.

The twins looked up the teacher's address in the telephone book in the office. The street wasn't too far away. They got on their bikes and pedaled out of the lumberyard.

When they found the small white house, the twins hopped off their bikes and headed up the front steps. Freddie rang the doorbell.

A short, plump man with gray hair came to the door. "Are you Mr. Berne? asked Flossie.

"Yes," the man said with a smile.

"We're trying to find out about your lessons," Freddie began. Mr. Berne nodded and started speaking quickly in French.

"No, no," Flossie said. "We want to know if a friend of ours is taking lessons here."

"His name is Sam," Freddie explained.

"Sam?" repeated Mr. Berne. He didn't seem to understand what they were saying.

"Wait," Flossie said, holding up her hand. She dug around in her pocket for her wallet. Then she pulled out a picture of Mr. Bobbsey and Sam, standing in front of the lumberyard. She pointed to Sam. "Do you know this man?" she asked.

The teacher's eyes lit up.

"Ah," he said. "Monsieur Johnson!" Then he began talking in French again.

"I think he's telling us how great Sam is at his lessons," Flossie whispered to Freddie.

"Well, he sure knows Sam," Freddie replied.

"Now we can prove where Sam was the night of the robbery."

The twins thanked Mr. Berne and waved. He was still waving back as they rode off on their bikes.

When Freddie and Flossie got back to the lumberyard, Bert and Nan were waiting for them.

"We were going to speak to Holly, but she isn't here," Bert told the younger twins.

"Dad told us she's at the university," Nan said.

"Let's go," Freddie said.

The twins rode their bikes to the campus and soon found the natural history building.

"Why isn't anybody around?" Nan asked as they entered the darkened building.

"Because there are no classes today!" a voice said.

The twins jumped. The voice seemed to come out of nowhere. They looked around.

"Over here," the voice said. The Bobbseys turned and saw a display case. Inside was a young man. He was carefully gluing fabric to the back of the case.

"We use the weekend to study and work on projects," the young man explained. "Like getting this case ready for a special exhibit. My class is studying owls. This exhibit will show what they eat."

"What *do* they eat?" asked Bert.

"Just about everything they can catch," the young man said cheerfully.

Nan shuddered and asked if he knew where Holly might be.

"Probably in one of those rooms at the end of the hall," he said. "They're for the paleontology students. At this end of the building we're interested in more modern animals."

The twins turned and headed for the end of the hallway. Halfway down, Freddie poked his head into one of the rooms.

"Hey!" he cried. "Look at all this stuff."

The other twins followed him inside. The room held rows of open shelves. On the shelves were bones, skulls, and lots of glass jars. The Bobbseys couldn't be sure of what the jars contained.

Flossie shivered and moved closer to Bert. "Let's get out of here," she said. "This place is spooky!"

Bert put his arm around her. "Don't worry, Floss. None of these things can hurt you."

Next they passed a room with huge pictures of dinosaur footprints lining the walls.

Finally they opened the next-to-the-last door on the corridor.

"Oh, wow," Nan whispered. "It's incredible."

Slowly the twins entered a huge room with a ceiling that was at least three stories high. They couldn't take their eyes off what filled the room—an enormous skeleton of a dinosaur. It reached from one end of the room to the other, and the head almost touched the ceiling. The twins looked at the skeleton more carefully. It was almost complete. Only the lower part of the right front leg was missing. In its place was a metal rod.

"This must be Professor Trent's Diplodocus," said Bert.

"It *is* pretty amazing," Nan admitted.

"It's pretty scary if you ask me," Flossie said with a shiver.

"You can understand why the professor got so upset at losing part of it," Freddie said.

"Let's keep looking for Holly," Nan said.

Carefully they closed the door, then checked

out the last room. Holly was sitting on a stool. She was holding a piece of a bone under a magnifying glass. On the counter in front of her was a model of a dinosaur.

"Holly!" Nan called.

Holly jumped. "Oh, it's you," she gasped. "What are you guys doing here?"

"Hey! Is that a Triceratops?" Freddie asked excitedly. "They're my favorite—"

"Actually, we're here to talk to you, Holly," Bert interrupted, giving Freddie a look.

"Right," said Nan. "We'd like to know where you were the night the bone was stolen."

"I was home," Holly said. "I mean, I was here. At a class." She fidgeted with the magnifying glass.

"What class?" Bert asked.

"I don't know," Holly snapped. "I mean, it was an archeology class."

"What time did the class get out?" Nan asked.

"Not late," Holly said.

The twins exchanged looks. Holly certainly seemed to have something to hide.

"Holly," Bert asked, "did you go back to the lumberyard that night and steal the bone after Chief dug it up?"

"No!" shouted Holly, jumping up. Then she burst into tears. "I can't stand it anymore," she said between sobs. "I'll tell you." She wiped the tears from her cheeks. "I buried the bone in the first place. I stole it from Professor Trent's lab!"

7

It's Only Fair . . .

"But why would you do that?" Flossie asked.

"You don't understand," Holly began.

Before Holly could say more, the door banged open. Standing there, glaring at them, was Professor Trent.

"Just what I suspected," he growled. "The five of you are in this together." He strode into the room. "This is just the sort of stuff I expected from you," he said to Holly.

Then Professor Trent turned to the twins. "I never believed you kids were trying to find my bone. You were just covering up what you did!"

"That's not true," Bert said. "We *are* trying to solve the mystery."

"There is no mystery," Professor Trent said. "Holly stole the bone, and you helped her."

Suddenly he reached out and grabbed Nan by the arm.

"You're going to tell me where that bone is hidden," he said. "Or else."

"You let go of her!" Bert shouted, starting toward him.

Professor Trent dropped Nan's arm. Nan quickly moved away.

Then Holly spoke up. "Leave these kids alone," she ordered Professor Trent. "I'm the one who took the bone. They had nothing to do with it. The first time they saw the bone was when Chief dug it up."

"So it *was* you," Professor Trent said. "I knew it."

"Then you also know why I took the bone, don't you?" Holly said. She looked the professor straight in the eye.

Professor Trent stared back at Holly. Then, to the twins' surprise, his shoulders slumped and he looked down at the floor. He didn't appear angry anymore. He looked ashamed.

"Are you going to tell them the whole story?" Holly asked.

Professor Trent didn't say anything.

"Then I'll tell them," Holly said. Professor Trent was still looking at the floor.

"Last summer I worked with Professor Trent on his dig," Holly explained. "He was hoping to find more dinosaur bones. Lots of other students also worked on the dig. Of course, Professor Trent is the expert, but the students have learned a lot. Some have been on digs before."

"That's true," Professor Trent muttered. He sounded very embarrassed.

"Professor Trent decided where we should dig," Holly continued. "He was sure that we would find dinosaur bones in the spot he had chosen."

Professor Trent raised his head. "I was in charge," he said. "It was my job to decide where we should dig."

"That's true," Holly admitted. "But I had an idea we weren't looking in the right place."

"But I had checked out that spot!" Professor Trent said. "I was positive it was the right place to dig."

"I know that you're an expert on dinosaurs,"

Holly said, "but this time you were wrong."

"So what did you do?" Nan asked Holly.

"After the day's work was over, I did my own digging. I went to the place that I thought we should be exploring," Holly explained. "After a few days some other students started to help me. A few weeks later we found a big piece of bone. It was part of a Diplodocus's leg." She looked at Professor Trent.

"So I sent over the whole crew, and we found the rest of the pieces," Professor Trent continued. "Then I took them back to the university and put them together. And then Holly stole the last bone I needed to make a complete skeleton."

"But you should have let people know you wouldn't have found the bone without me," Holly said quietly. "It was mine."

"No," Professor Trent said. "It's my dinosaur. That bone is just part of it."

"Well, that doesn't seem very fair," Freddie said. "After all, Holly did figure out where to look."

"So she should get the credit," Bert said.

"This isn't a treasure hunt," Professor Trent said. "This is science."

"But I'm a scientist, too!" Holly burst out.

"It was my expedition," the professor pointed out.

"But *I* found the bone," Holly insisted.

The two of them glared at each other.

"All this arguing won't solve anything," Bert said.

"Yeah," said Freddie. "Aren't you tired of fighting with each other all the time?"

"But I've been working on that skeleton for ten years," Professor Trent said. "Finishing it is the most important thing in the world to me."

"I know," Holly said. "I wanted to help you finish the skeleton. But I also want people to know that I did something important."

Holly turned to the twins. "Can you understand that?"

"But why did you steal the bone?" Nan asked. "You wanted to finish the skeleton, too."

"It seemed to be the only way to make Professor Trent listen to me," Holly said.

The twins turned and looked at the professor. He was staring at the model of the Triceratops. Finally he looked at Holly and said, "I'm sorry, Holly. I promise I'll tell people what you did. It's only fair. You're an excellent student."

There were tears in Holly's eyes. "Thanks," she whispered.

"So now will you give me back the bone?" Professor Trent asked.

Holly shook her head. "I told you," she said. "I don't have it. I stole it the first time and buried it in the lumberyard. But I have no idea where it is now. This time a real thief took it!"

8

Strange
Happenings
at the Zoo

When the twins got back home, they discussed the case over a snack of milk and cookies.

"I believed Holly," Nan said. "Didn't you?"

The other twins nodded. "So she wasn't the one who stole the bone out of Dad's office," Freddie said.

"And we found out that Sam was at his French lesson," Flossie said. "He didn't do it, either."

"Why don't we find out what Dr. Hayes was doing the night of the robbery," Bert suggested. "She's the most likely suspect."

"Why do you say that?" Nan said.

"Because of the strange way she disappeared from the office the other day," Bert said. "And we haven't heard from her since. You'd think she'd want to know more about the bone."

"We have no proof that Dr. Hayes had anything to do with the bone," Nan said.

"Well, who do *you* suspect?" Bert asked.

"What about Professor Trent?" Nan said. "He might have stolen his own bone back just to teach Holly a lesson."

"I don't know," Bert said. "He seems awfully upset for somebody who really does know where the bone is."

"That's true," Nan admitted. "But that still doesn't mean Willa Hayes is the thief."

"So let's go to the zoo and find out," Bert said.

"I think I'll go to the lumberyard to search for clues," Nan said. "Maybe we missed something there."

"I'm going with Nan," Flossie announced.

"I'll go with you, Bert," Freddie said. "Even if we don't find anything, it'll be fun."

"I think I'll phone Dr. Hayes to make sure she's there," Bert said.

Bert called Dr. Hayes on the phone. "My

brother and I would like to come to your office in a little while," he told her. "We're still investigating the missing dinosaur bone, and we need some expert advice."

"I'm sorry, Bert," Dr. Hayes replied. "But I don't have time to talk to you today."

"But—" Bert began.

"I really have to go now," interrupted Dr. Hayes. She hung up the phone.

"That's pretty suspicious," Freddie said to his sisters, after Bert repeated the conversation.

The twins finished their snack. Then Freddie and Bert rode their bikes to the zoo. It was close to five o'clock. Soon the zoo would be closing for the day. It took the boys a little while to find Dr. Hayes's office. They knocked loudly on the door, but nobody answered.

"I wonder where she is," Bert said.

"She has to be around here somewhere," Freddie said.

The brothers began searching the zoo. There was a big crowd around the seal pool. Everyone was watching the seals play in the water.

The boys walked through the lion and tiger house, but they didn't see Dr. Hayes there, either.

"Come on, Freddie," Bert said. He tugged at

his younger brother's arm. "Let's keep looking."

"Just a minute," Freddie said. "I want to see the tigers."

"You can come back another time," Bert said firmly. "Remember, we're on an important case."

When they got to the monkey house, Freddie had to remind Bert that they were at the zoo on serious business.

But at the hall of reptiles, Freddie slowed down again.

"Look at that," he said. He stopped in front of the tank holding a dragon lizard. "His ancestors lived on the earth millions of years ago. They're related to dinosaurs, you know."

Bert rolled his eyes. "I know, I know," he said. "Come on, we have to find Dr. Hayes."

Finally, they spotted her near the bear cages.

"Careful," Bert said. He stepped behind a hot dog stand and pulled Freddie next to him. "Don't let her see us."

Dr. Hayes walked up to a security guard who was keeping a watchful eye on the crowd. Bert and Freddie were close enough to hear what she said to him.

"It's almost closing time, Henry," Dr. Hayes said. "Please make sure that everyone leaves here as soon as the zoo closes. I want this area completely cleared."

"Yes, ma'am," the guard said.

"Good," Dr. Hayes said, and she walked away.

"Let's follow her," Bert said.

The two boys slipped quietly from building to building. They tried to stay in the middle of crowds so that Dr. Hayes wouldn't see them. That was hard to do because everyone was beginning to move toward the gates of the zoo. But Dr. Hayes was going in the opposite direction.

"She must be heading for her office," Bert told Freddie. "Stay close behind her."

Just as Dr. Hayes got to the front of the administration building, Bert and Freddie heard footsteps behind them. They quickly ducked behind the corner of the building.

Two men wearing coveralls came walking up to the entrance of the building. Dr. Hayes was waiting in the doorway for them.

"Finally," the boys heard her say. "I was worried you wouldn't be here in time to set things up."

"Sorry," one of the men said. "There were complications."

"When you have to sneak around, things take longer," the other man added with a laugh.

"But you do have it," Dr. Hayes said.

"Yep. It's safe as can be," said the first man.

"Good," said Willa Hayes. "Why don't you come into my office. We'll make the final arrangements."

The three of them went inside. Freddie and Bert stared at each other.

"Wow!" said Freddie. "Willa Hayes really *is* our thief. But why did she steal the bone?"

"Well, it's very valuable to zoologists like Dr. Hayes," Bert pointed out. "Maybe she wants to have a special exhibit at the zoo."

"We'd better call the police right away," said Freddie. "They're the only ones who can stop her now."

The two boys crept closer to the edge of the building. Bert peered around the corner.

"It's okay," he whispered to Freddie. "The coast is clear."

"Mphhhhhh," said Freddie.

"What?" said Bert. Suddenly he felt a huge hand grab him tightly by the shoulder.

9

A New Clue

Slowly Bert turned his head. Standing behind him was Henry, the zoo guard. Henry's other hand was on Freddie's shoulder.

"Let's go, kids," the guard said with a smile. "Don't you know that it's closing time?"

"But we haven't seen everything yet," Freddie said quickly.

"That's okay," Henry said. "You can always come back another time. The animals have to get their rest." The guard's voice was very nice, but he kept his hands on the boys' shoulders. He began to move them quickly toward the path that led away from Dr. Hayes's office.

Before Bert and Freddie could say anything else, the door to the building opened. Willa Hayes stood on the top step. She hurried over to them.

"Henry, I can't work with all of this noise," Dr. Hayes said. She sounded very annoyed. "What's going on here?"

"I found these two kids wandering around," the guard explained. "I was just explaining to them that it's time to go home."

"You don't have to hold on to them anymore," Dr. Hayes told Henry. "I know these boys." The guard removed his hands from the Bobbseys' shoulders.

Dr. Hayes turned to Bert and Freddie. "I told you that I was too busy to talk to you today," she said. "What are you doing here? I'd like an explanation."

"So would we," Freddie shot back. "You can't fool us. We know you stole our dinosaur bone, and we want it back!"

"Well, actually, it's Professor Trent's bone," Bert put in quickly. "He should be the one to display it. And it should be in a museum, not in a zoo!"

Willa Hayes stared at them angrily. "You

know, you kids should be more careful about accusing people of things," she said. "Especially when you don't have proof. And maybe you should learn to mind your own business!"

With that, Dr. Hayes turned and walked back up to the administration building. She slammed the door behind her.

"Come on, you two," Henry said. "I want you guys out of here. Now."

The guard escorted the boys to the front gate. He didn't take his eyes off them until they were on their bikes and heading away from the zoo.

The minute they got home, Bert and Freddie raced to find their sisters. They told Nan and Flossie everything they had seen and heard at the zoo.

"So, it *is* Dr. Hayes," Freddie finished excitedly. "She's the one who stole the bone."

"But you don't really know that for sure," Flossie said.

"You should have been there," Freddie said. "She wouldn't tell us *anything*."

"She *was* acting very strangely," Bert added. "As if she had something to hide."

"But you still don't have any proof," Nan pointed out. "I mean, she didn't *say* anything about the bone?"

"Well, no," Freddie admitted. "But we'll get proof."

"*We* found a whole new clue," Flossie said proudly.

"What did you find?" asked Bert.

"We searched the lumberyard again very carefully," Nan said. "And we found another place where the ground was dug up. It was also near the fence."

"Did you find anything in the ground?" asked Bert.

"We didn't have time to do any digging," Nan said. "We found the hole just as the lumberyard was closing."

"So you don't have any proof, either," Bert pointed out.

"That's why we're going back tomorrow," Nan told him. "To find out."

"We're going to bring Chief, too," Flossie added. "We're going to let him search the lumberyard. Maybe he'll find a clue that we missed."

Bert shrugged. "You know, that's not a bad idea."

"We'll come, too," Freddie said to Bert. "Then afterward Flossie and Nan can help us find proof that Dr. Hayes was the real thief."

The next afternoon, after school, the twins headed for the lumberyard once again on their bikes. Chief happily trotted along behind them.

When they got to Mr. Bobbsey's office, Flossie picked up the cloth they had used to wipe off the bone after Chief had dug it up.

"This cloth has the smell of the bone on it," she said. "Chief will pick up the scent and lead us to something." She held the cloth under Chief's nose.

"Smell," she commanded. Freddie and Bert burst out laughing.

Nan and Flossie ignored them. So did Chief. In fact, as soon as Chief sniffed the cloth, his tail started wagging.

"Now go find some clues," Flossie told him.

Chief yelped and bounded out of the office. Flossie had a hard time trying to hold on to his leash.

He led the twins through the lumberyard. He dragged Flossie over and around several piles of lumber. It was hard, but Flossie held on tightly.

Finally Chief stopped near the back fence.

"Look!" Flossie pointed. "It's the place we found yesterday."

"That's right," Nan said. "See? You can tell that somebody has been digging here."

Flossie unsnapped Chief's leash. The sheepdog began circling the hole, with all four Bobbseys following. Then Chief stopped and began sniffing at the ground.

Suddenly he gave a yelp and began to dig frantically. Soon all the twins could see of him was the tip of his tail. He growled and started digging even harder.

"What's going on there, boy?" Bert asked the dog. He tried to peer into the hole, but he couldn't see a thing.

Moments later Chief began to back out of the hole.

"He's coming out," Nan said.

"He found something!" Flossie cried. She was jumping up and down.

A minute later Chief backed out of the hole. He was dragging something in his mouth. Something large and covered with dirt.

"Look!" Nan exclaimed.

"I can't believe it!" said Freddie.

"He found the bone!" cheered Flossie.

10

Caught in the Act

Bert wrestled the bone away from Chief and wiped it off with the cloth.

"There!" Flossie cried. "That proves Dr. Hayes is innocent. She couldn't have taken the bone to the zoo because it's still here!"

"I guess you're right," Freddie said. He sounded disappointed. "Then who *did* bury the bone?"

"Holly could have buried it after Chief dug it up," Bert said. "Maybe she lied when she told us she didn't know where it was."

"What about Professor Trent?" Nan asked. "He could have stolen the bone and buried it to get Holly into trouble."

"But he said he was sorry. And he promised to tell that she found the bone in the first place," Freddie pointed out.

"And we know that Sam and Dr. Hayes are innocent," Flossie added. "So what are we going to do now?"

"I know," Nan said. "Let's recreate the crime!"

"Great idea!" said Freddie.

"We might notice a clue we missed in all the excitement," said Bert.

"Let's do exactly what we did the first time Chief dug up the bone," Flossie said.

"I better go find Sam and Dad," Freddie said. "They should be in on this, too."

In a minute Freddie returned, followed by Sam and Mr. Bobbsey. On the way back to the office, the twins explained the plan.

Just as they reached the door, Holly appeared. "You found it!" she cried. She sounded really excited.

"Yes," said Nan. "And now we're going to find out who stole it."

Holly reached out to take the bone. Then a customer came up and asked her for help, and she had to go.

After everyone was inside the office, Nan

closed the door. "Holly really looked like she wanted to grab the bone just now." Nan frowned. "Maybe she is the one, after all."

"But Holly wasn't here the day we found the bone," Bert reminded Nan.

"That's right," Sam said. "She doesn't work Fridays."

"We didn't *see* her," Nan pointed out. "But she could have been here anyway. Let's keep an eye on her."

"Now we have to call the zoo," Flossie said.

Bert dialed the number and asked for Dr. Hayes. He spoke to her for a minute and then hung up.

"I told her we found the bone. She sounded real glad, but she said she can't come to see it until tomorrow," Bert reported. "What's next?"

"After we called the zoo, we went back to the hole," Freddie said. "To take pictures."

"I think we can skip that part," Bert said. "We want to know what happened *after* we left the bone here."

"Here's the box," Flossie said.

The twins carefully put the bone into the cardboard box. Then they covered the box with the ripped lid.

The twins, Mr. Bobbsey, Sam, and Chief all piled out of the office and headed for the lumberyard gate. Sam reached in his pockets, searching for his keys.

"Wait!" said Flossie. "This was when I realized Freddie lost my camera."

"Right," said Bert. "And we all looked for it."

"Everybody should go back now and search the same places that they did that night," Nan said.

Flossie bent over to pet Chief. "We'll be right back," she promised the dog. "You wait here for us, okay?"

By now the others had begun to spread out. Flossie ran to catch up with them and promptly tripped over a piece of lumber.

"Ouch!" she said, falling to the ground.

When Flossie tried to get up, her eyes filled with tears. I twisted my ankle, she told herself. She didn't cry, but her ankle hurt too much to walk. She sat down next to a stack of boards to wait for her ankle to stop throbbing.

Then Flossie heard the office door creak open. Carefully she peered around the pile of lumber. She stood up and silently crept closer, trying to ignore the pain in her ankle.

From inside the office she could hear a scraping sound. The thief! Forgetting about her ankle, Flossie lunged forward.

"Everyone come back! Hurry!" Flossie yelled.

The other twins, Sam, and Mr. Bobbsey came running. Holly hurried over from another part of the lumberyard.

When they got to the office, Flossie and Chief were sitting together on the ground. The bone was lying in front of them.

"Are you all right?" asked Mr. Bobbsey.

"I twisted my ankle," Flossie said. "But that doesn't matter now."

"Where's the thief?" asked Freddie.

"Right here," Flossie said with a big smile. She gave Chief a pat on the head.

"Chief stole the bone?" asked Freddie.

"But how could he get through the locked door?" Nan said.

"Wait a minute," said Bert. "The door wasn't locked. Freddie looked in the office for the camera, remember? Then we all went off to search for it. That was before Sam had a chance to lock the door."

"So Chief took the bone when we were looking for Flossie's camera!" said Nan.

"We know who buried the bone the first time," said Bert.

"And now we know who buried it the second time." Freddie glared at Chief.

"But why was Dr. Hayes acting so strangely?" Bert wondered.

"I don't know," said Nan. "But I think we should call Professor Trent and tell him his dinosaur bone is safe."

"I'll call," said Holly. "After all, none of this would have happened if I hadn't taken the bone in the first place."

Mr. Bobbsey carried Flossie into the office and put her down on his chair. The others all crowded around the desk. But before Holly could make the call, the phone rang.

Mr. Bobbsey answered it. "Hello," he said. "Yes, Dr. Hayes, they're right here. Why, yes. They did catch the thief."

Bert took the phone and told Dr. Hayes about the results of the investigation. Then he listened for a minute. "We sure would!" he exclaimed. "Thanks very much!"

Bert hung up and turned to the others. "Guess what?" Lakeport Zoo just got a brand-new polar bear. The bear is still pretty young.

Dr. Hayes wanted to move it into the zoo as quietly as possible. That's why she was being so mysterious. She wanted the bear to get used to its new home before people came to see it. She invited us to be among the first to see the bear!"

"That sounds great!" cheered Flossie.

"And I'm going to give you a special tour of the natural history building—if it's all right with Professor Trent," Holly said.

"That's for me!" crowed Freddie.

"When I call the professor," Holly continued, "I'm going to ask if I can work with him again. I still have a lot to learn."

She leaned over to pet the dog. "Thanks, Chief. You saved our dinosaur." The sheepdog looked a little sad. "I know how you feel," Holly told him. "I once stole and lost a dinosaur bone myself."

Everybody laughed.

"I'd like to help build Chief's new home," Holly told the twins. "That is, if you could use the help."

"We sure could," said Freddie. "It's about time we got back to building that doghouse."

"Your new home will cheer you up, Chief," Flossie told the dog.

"And I'm going to bring you a wonderful new bone for a housewarming present," Holly promised.

Chief barked happily.

Nan smiled. "I think that's just what he'd like!"

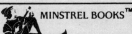